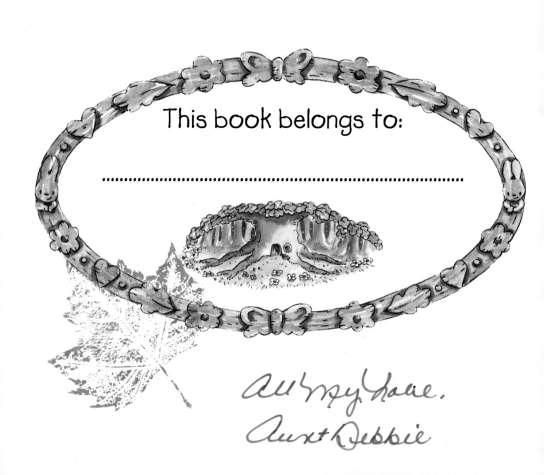

This book belongs to:

....

All My Love,
Aunt Debbie

The naughty bunny

A little bunny story

PaRRagon

Bath · New York · Singapore · Hong Kong · Cologne · Delhi · Melbourne

Four little bunnies live under the roots of a big, old oak tree in Dingle Wood.

This is Fern.

This is Daisy.

This is Blackberry.

And this is Rocky.

Rocky is a naughty little bunny who is always getting into trouble.

This is Rocky's story.

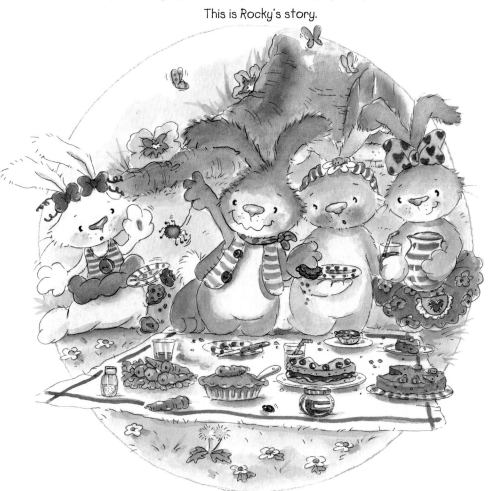

Early one morning, Rocky and the other little bunnies were snuggled up in their cozy beds deep inside Bunny Burrow.

Outside, a strong wind was blowing.

The branches of the big, old oak tree swayed from side to side. Its leaves were swooshing and swishing everywhere!

The wind grew stronger and stronger.

Then, it blew straight into the burrow, right into the bunnies'
bedroom! It whistled around, rattling doors, knocking
books onto the floor, and waking all the bunnies.

Blackberry pulled her sheet up and said, in a worried voice,
"I hope it won't be windy at the Woodland Parade—it will blow our hats off!"

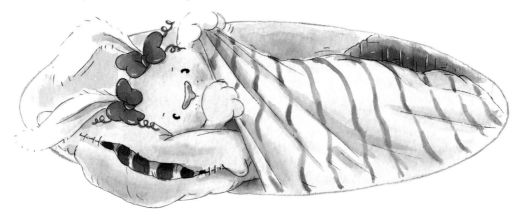

Daisy peeped through one eye and whispered,
"Oh! I'd forgotten all about the Woodland Parade!"

Fern twitched her nose and said,
"We've got a lot to do to get
our hats ready for the parade—
we'll all have to help each other!"

The whistling wind didn't bother Rocky.
"I'm so excited!" he cried, hopping out of bed.
"I'll go and collect things to make our hats. It will be so much fun!"

As Rocky hopped out of bed, the wind knocked him off his feet
and rolled him into a ball.

Then, it blew him outside!

"Tee, hee!" giggled Rocky.
"That was great!"

Rocky picked himself up and looked around.
Everyone was busy getting ready for the parade.

Mrs. Bumble was straightening her wings. Fergie Frog was
washing his hands. Monty Mouse was brushing his
teeth and Sammy Squirrel was combing his big, bushy tail.

"Oh, Rocky!" said Mrs. Bumble.
"You're covered in leaves—you can't go to the parade like that!"

Rocky looked down and saw that he was covered in leaves from
head to tail! He bounced up and down and shook himself clean.
"That's better!" he cried.

Later that day, Rocky remembered that he had promised
to help make the hats for the parade.

Hopping past Mrs. Bumble's yard, he saw some pretty
sunflowers. "They will make the hats really special," he thought.

So, while Mrs. Bumble was busy watering her plants, Rocky crawled under the fence and grabbed some of her flowers!

Then, the naughty bunny decided to carry on collecting things that didn't belong to him.

He grabbed some twigs from Sammy Squirrel's fence...

... stole some nuts from Monty's mouse hole...

... and even took one of Fergie Frog's water lily pads from Lily Pond.

Soon, Rocky had collected everything he needed to help make some really special hats.

"Everyone will think the wind blew these things away!"
giggled the naughty bunny. "No one will know I took them!"

Back inside the burrow, the other bunnies were helping each other make the hats for the parade. What a mess they'd made! The floor was covered in buds and bows, leaves and flowers.

"Rocky, where have you been?" asked Blackberry. "It's nearly time for the parade and we haven't even started making my hat!"

Suddenly, Blackberry noticed puddles of water on the floor.

"What have you been up to, you naughty bunny?" she asked.

"I've been collecting special things for the hats," said Rocky. "Look!" and he held out his paws.

"Where did you get those pretty flowers from?" asked Daisy.

"And those twigs?" said Fern.

"And where did you find those nuts and the water lily pad?" said Blackberry.

Rocky's nose started to twitch. He shuffled his feet on
the floor and said, "Er... the wind blew them into my paws!"

Suddenly, there was a knock at the door of the burrow. The bunnies pricked up their ears.

"Come in!" they called.

The door opened and there stood a cross Monty Mouse, an unhappy Fergie Frog, an annoyed Sammy Squirrel, and a very upset Mrs. Bumble.

"Rocky!" said Fergie Frog, sternly. "You've been taking things that don't belong to you."

Rocky's nose twitched
even more and he began
to look unhappy.

"Oh, Rocky. You haven't been naughty, have you?" asked Blackberry.

"Yes, he has," said Fergie.
"We've all lost something today.
We thought it was the wind until we saw a trail
of puddles leading into Dingle Wood.

"We followed the trail and it led us here. There's only one naughty bunny that lives in Bunny Burrow. That's Rocky!"

"I'm sorry," said Rocky. "I just wanted to help make some really special hats."

"But it's wrong to take things that don't belong to you," said Fergie, firmly.

"I promise I won't do it again," said Rocky. He gave the water lily pad back to Fergie Frog, the twigs to Sammy Squirrel, the nuts to Monty Mouse, and the flowers to Mrs. Bumble.

The animals soon forgave Rocky and they went back home.

Fern and Daisy put on their hats and, with Blackberry, set off
for the Woodland Parade. Rocky stayed behind.

"I'll meet you there," he called after them.

What was the naughty bunny up to this time?

As soon as the others were
out of sight, Rocky started
making a hat for Blackberry
to wear at the parade.
But, this time he used an old
woolly hat and his special shiny
button collection.

As soon as he'd finished, Rocky raced to the parade
to give Blackberry her hat.

"Oh, thank you," said Bramble. "It's the prettiest hat I've ever seen!"

So Rocky, the naughty bunny, and his three friends looked the smartest little bunnies
at the windy Woodland Parade.